SEVEN·WAYS·to·TRICK·A·TROLL

Seven·Ways·to·Trick·a·Troll

···Lise Lunge·Larsen···
···Illustrations by Kari Vick···

 University of Minnesota Press

Minneapolis ◆ London

To Espen—may you outwit every troll you meet on life's journey!
—L.L.L.

For Mom, the epitome of grace and courage, and Dad, who taught me to see.
—K.V.

Published by the University of Minnesota Press
111 Third Avenue South, Suite 290
Minneapolis, MN 55401-2520
http://www.upress.umn.edu

ISBN: 978-0-8166-9977-3 (hc)
A Cataloging-in-Publication record for this book is available from the Library of Congress.

Printed in China

The University of Minnesota is an equal-opportunity educator and employer.

23 22 21 20 19 18 17   10 9 8 7 6 5 4 3 2 1

Contents

Introduction

Just what are trolls? If you listen to the stories of the ancient Norse, you learn that trolls were among the first things on Earth. In fact, the very world we live in was created from the father of all trolls, an enormous frost giant named Ymir. The original trolls crawled out from between his toes. This happened at the beginning of time, before there were humans, before there even was an Earth.

That's because the Earth was made from Ymir's body. He was that big! His bones and teeth became mountains and rocks, and his hair became trees, shrubs, and grass. His blood turned into oceans, lakes, and rivers. His skull became the vault of the sky and his brains became the clouds. No wonder the ancients saw trolls everywhere. Their world was made from troll parts!

The very first trolls, the ones who crept out from between Ymir's toes, had six heads and six arms. Later trolls came in different sizes and shapes, some with only one head, others with several. Some had tails, some didn't. All of them were huge and hated humans when we came along.

Luckily for us, their brains were tiny, only about the size of a walnut, which meant that even small children could trick a troll as long as they knew the trolls' weaknesses and remembered not to be afraid.

It is said that there are two kinds of stories: the one about the stranger you go and seek, the other about the stranger who arrives at your door. The stranger can be a person, a storm, a disaster, a death, an opportunity, an elf, a dragon, or even a troll. The point is that in this encounter the story happens. It will always be a struggle. It will change you in some way, or maybe it changes the landscape you live in. The result can be an insight, a new strength revealed, a changed attitude, a new rock formation, or a new flower. Whatever it is, it's a change.

Troll stories set this encounter into sharp focus. Nothing is stranger or inspires more fear than trolls because they seek our demise and hate everything we stand for. They in turn stand for all that is evil and ugly. When we act in ways that are unkind, we are letting our latent troll nature take over.

Troll stories put the struggle between good and evil into a narrative that is entertaining as well as enlightening. Through these tales we see that although trolls are fearsome, they are not very bright and they can be tricked. But that is no easy matter. To defeat a troll, you must draw on the very best of your humanity: you must have courage, patience, intelligence, kindness, the ability to work with others, and plenty of moxie. It also helps to know a troll's weaknesses, and that's where this book comes in. On the surface this is an entertaining collection of stories, but it's equally a book that helps us discover that we have the tools to deal with difficult challenges in life.

So read on, and you too will be prepared to trick a troll!

Troll Weakness One

Trolls hate loud noise, especially the sound of bells.

◆ ◆ ◆

Trolls can have several heads. This makes them especially hideous to look at and confusing to listen to because sometimes the heads talk at the same time. These many-headed trolls are prone to unbearable headaches brought on by loud noise. This is to your advantage.

Little Goose

Once upon a time there was a little girl who lived with her mother in a village at the foot of a mountain far north in a country called Norway. The girl tended her mother's geese, and because she was quite small for her age and also full of silly tricks, everyone called her Little Goose.

Little Goose's village was a quiet, pleasant place except for one thing—a terrible troll lived in the nearby mountains. He wasn't as tall as many trolls but frightfully broad, and he had three heads and six enormous ears! For hundreds of years he had stolen gold and silver from the people who lived in the nearby villages. And at night he sometimes trampled down the vegetables and the grain. Other times he frightened the horses and the cows and stole sheep and pigs for his dinner. Worst of all, he gobbled up any villager who was unlucky enough to be out in the mountains at night.

One bright summer day Little Goose decided to go up into the mountains to pick cloudberries, her favorite berry.

"No," said her mom. "You cannot go. What if the terrible troll catches you?"

But Little Goose knew that trolls were only out at night, so when her mom wasn't looking, she snuck off.

Up in the mountains plump berries gleamed like gold coins as far as her eye could see. In no time she had filled her basket and her pockets. Then she began to eat. She ate berries until her stomach ached and she was too tired to move. Wrapping her warm feather cloak around her, she stretched out in the heather to rest. Soon she was fast asleep.

When she awoke, it was dark. Little Goose looked and looked for the trail to the village, but no matter how she searched, she could not find it. Finally she came upon a cave and decided to stay there till morning.

All around the creatures of the night began to stir. A wolf howled, an owl screeched, and the wind blew mournfully through the pines. After a while she heard another kind of sound: snorting and snuffling. Then a huge shape rose before her. It was the terrible troll.

"Who's in my cave?" growled the troll.

"It . . . it . . . it's just me," stammered Little Goose.

"Who are you?"

"I'm Little Goose."

"You're a strange looking goose! You almost look like a small person, but of course people don't have feathers," he grunted, one of his heads peering at Little Goose's cloak. "Luckily for you, I don't eat geese or chickens. The feathers get stuck in my teeth."

Little Goose relaxed a little and the troll, feeling chatty, rumbled on.

"You know, people never come here. They fear me more than anything because I love to eat them," he boasted. "Tell me, Little Goose, is there anything you are afraid of?" he asked.

"I'm . . . I'm scared of gold," said Little Goose. It was the first thing that popped into her head.

"That is the silliest thing I ever heard. I love gold. I have heaps of it! Maybe I'll fetch some just to scare you."

"Oh, don't do that," whimpered Little Goose, pretending to be frightened. "Gold blinds my eyes. And if I touch it, it burns and blisters my skin!"

Feeling braver and also very curious, Little Goose asked, "Is there anything you are scared of?"

"I hate loud noises," the troll confessed. "Especially bells and whistles. The ringing makes all my three heads pound and my ears ring for weeks and weeks so I can't sleep or hunt or do anything."

The troll went on describing his horror of loud noises and the places he had to leave because of it. Toward morning he muttered, "I have to go," and disappeared deeper into the cave.

Little Goose ran outside. When the sun rose, she found the trail and dashed straight for home.

"Oh, Little Goose, where have you been? I was so worried!" cried her mom.

"I have been with the terrible troll, and now I know how we can get rid of him," she told her mom.

The very next evening, the villagers marched off, Little Goose leading the way. When they reached the cave everyone brought out their bells, whistles, drums, pots, and pans. They rang, blew, drummed, and clanged as loud as they could.

"AHHHRRRRG!" bellowed a voice from inside the mountain, and the troll stormed out of the cave, hands over his ears. When he saw Little Goose, his many eyes blazed in fury.

"I'm going to get you for this, Little Goose," he roared and ran off.

The next night, Little Goose and her mother double-bolted the door. Toward midnight, loud thumping and snorting erupted outside.

A window shattered and the troll's middle head glared in.

"Now I'll have my revenge on you. You shall feel how dreadful it is to face what you are most afraid of," he snarled. Little Goose squeezed her eyes shut, expecting to feel sharp teeth. Instead a crash and a whoosh sent her sprawling as an enormous sack landed on the floor. It split open and gold poured out.

When Little Goose saw that, she laughed until her sides ached. She had tricked the terrible troll. He had believed her when she said she was afraid of gold!

The troll never came back to his cave in the mountain because now the villagers knew his secret. But to be safe, they built a bell tower in the town square. And every year they held a cloudberry festival to celebrate Little Goose who helped rid them of the terrible troll.

Troll Weakness Two

Trolls burst if they get too mad.

◆ ◆ ◆

Trolls are thieves. They steal gold, silver, jewels, and all kinds of valuables from humans. They can live for hundreds of years, so they gather a lot of treasure, which they hide inside their mountain homes. They also have short tempers. If you are good at teasing, you might make a troll so angry that he bursts, and then you might get some treasure back.

The Ashlad Who Stole the Troll's Treasures

Once upon a time there were three brothers whose parents died, leaving them nothing but an old wooden trough.

"What a useless piece of junk," scoffed Peter and Paul, the two eldest brothers. They set off for the king's farm, where Peter got a job working for the gardener and Paul for the coachman. The youngest, nicknamed Espen Ashlad because he liked to sit around and poke in the ashes, looked at the trough and thought, "Who knows? It may come in handy one day." He hoisted it on his back and trudged off after his brothers.

The Ashlad was so sooty and dirty that nobody at the king's farm would hire him. But his manners were good and his arms strong, so the cook let him haul water and wood to the kitchen.

Once he had a bath, Espen Ashlad turned out to be handsome. What's more, he always lent a helping hand where it was needed, and it didn't take long before all the maids began to favor him.

Peter and Paul did not like that one bit.

It just so happened that the king's farm was by a lake and on the opposite side lived a troll who had stolen seven silver ducks from the king's grandfather. The king longed to have the ducks back, but he dared not fetch them for he was terribly afraid of the troll.

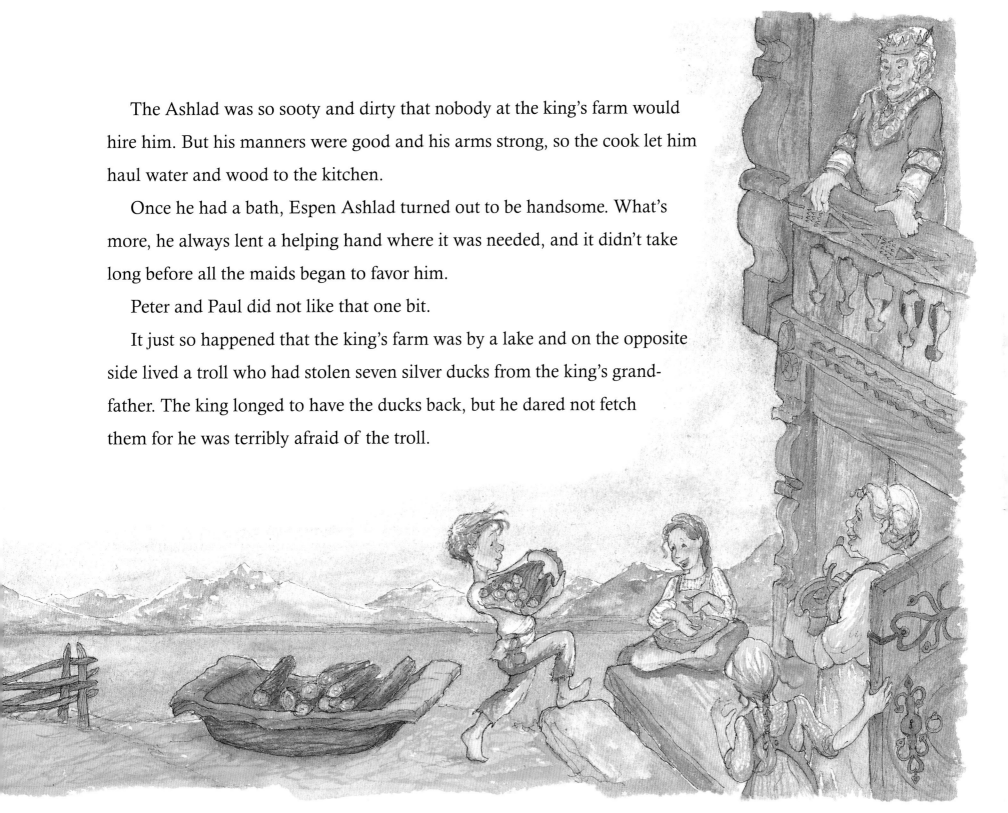

Peter and Paul went to the king and told him, "Our brother has been bragging that he can get the troll's seven silver ducks."

The king nearly jumped out of his chair with excitement and demanded the Ashlad do as he had boasted.

"Give me a bucket of grain and I will see what I can do," the boy said.

Using the trough as a boat, he rowed across the lake. On the beach the ducks waddled around, their silver feathers sparkling.

"Here, ducky, ducky!" cooed the Ashlad and sprinkled a line of grain straight into the trough and rowed away with the ducks.

When the king received the ducks he was so pleased that he promoted the Ashlad to groundskeeper. Peter and Paul were green with envy. Soon they went back to the king.

"Our brother has been bragging again. He says he's good for stealing the troll's bedspread, the one that has silver and gold squares."

"Oh, that belonged to my grandmother," exclaimed the king, who then called the Ashlad.

"You've said it and now you must do it," the king commanded.

Shaking his head, Espen sighed, "I'll try."

He rowed across in his trough, and this time he hid behind some large bushes. Soon the troll's daughter came out and hung the bedspread on a line to air out. When the troll daughter turned her back, the Ashlad grabbed the bedspread and rowed away.

Now the king made the Ashlad his personal servant. Peter and Paul were furious and went to the king.

"Our brother has been boasting that he can get the golden harp from the troll, the one that makes whoever listens happy regardless of how sad he is."

"Oh! That belonged to my great-grandfather," said the king, and he called the Ashlad.

"You said it and now you have to do it," he ordered.

"All right, but I'll need a week to plan," insisted the Ashlad.

At week's end he tucked a tenpenny nail, a birch stick, and a candle stump in his pocket and rowed off. On the other side he hid the trough and began to walk up and down the beach.

"Ho! Did you take my silver ducks?" bellowed the troll when he caught sight of the Ashlad.

"Yes, I did," said the lad.

"Did you also take my bedspread with the gold and silver squares?"

"I did."

"Well, now you're mine," shouted the troll and grabbed him.

"Daughter," called the troll. "I have caught the fellow who stole our treasures. Put him in the fattening coop and give him plenty to eat. When he's good and fat, we'll cook him and have a feast."

"Yes, Father," drooled the troll daughter.

Every day she brought the Ashlad roasted meat, sausages, hams, puddings, cakes, and pies. After eight days, the troll said, "Daughter, make a cut in his little finger and see if he's ready." But the Ashlad stuck out the nail and she cut that instead.

"He's as hard as iron," complained the troll daughter.

"Keep feeding him then," grunted the troll.

Eight days later the troll daughter returned. This time the Ashlad stuck out the birch stick.

"He's still as tough as wood," fretted the daughter.

"Keep feeding him then," grumbled the troll.

When the eight days were up, the troll daughter demanded, "Out with your little finger." This time he put out the candle stump.

"Now he's fine," she cackled.

"Good. I'll invite the guests. Meanwhile, you must prepare him. I want one half roasted and the other half boiled," the troll declared and strode out of the mountain.

The troll daughter brought out a great long knife, which she began to sharpen.

"Is that the knife you're going to use?" asked the Ashlad.

"Yes, it is," answered she.

"But you're not sharpening it right. I'll show you how to do it."

After he had sharpened the knife, the Ashlad said, "Let's try it on one of your braids."

He grabbed the troll daughter's hair and laughed, "Now you are *my* prisoner. Into the fattening coop you go!"

When she was locked up, the Ashlad ordered, "Give me your clothes."

The troll daughter took off her dress, apron, and even her kerchief so she was left in nothing but her underwear!

Outside the Ashlad found a cow, which he prepared, and when all was ready he dressed himself in the troll daughter's clothes.

Soon enough the troll returned with the guests. Looking at what he thought was his daughter, the troll boomed, "Come here and join us in this fine feast."

"I don't care to eat today. I feel so sad and downcast," quavered the Ashlad, his voice sounding like the troll's daughter.

"You know the cure for that. Just get the gold harp and play a little."

"I have forgotten where it is," confessed the Ashlad.

"It's where you left it, on the ledge above the door."

At once the Ashlad fetched the harp and played a few tunes. The trolls began to sing and laugh loudly. While they feasted, the Ashlad slipped away.

After a bit, the troll noticed his daughter was missing. When he found her in the fattening coop, he understood what had happened. Both trolls ran outside and spotted the Ashlad far out on the lake.

"You!" fumed the troll. "You took my silver ducks and my bedspread with the silver and gold squares!"

"Yes, I did!" chuckled the Ashlad.

"And now you have taken my golden harp also?"

"Yes, I have," laughed the Ashlad.

"Didn't I eat you then?" raged the troll.

"No! That was your own cow you ate," replied the Ashlad triumphantly.

The troll and his daughter jumped up and down, shook their fists, and flew into such a fury that they burst. The explosion created a wave that sent the Ashlad and his trough far up the shore on the other side of the lake.

When the king received the golden harp, he was so excited he made the Ashlad his chief steward in charge of the entire farm.

And they all lived happily till the end of their days because the Ashlad treated everyone well, even his brothers. He believed they had only meant to help him when they said those things.

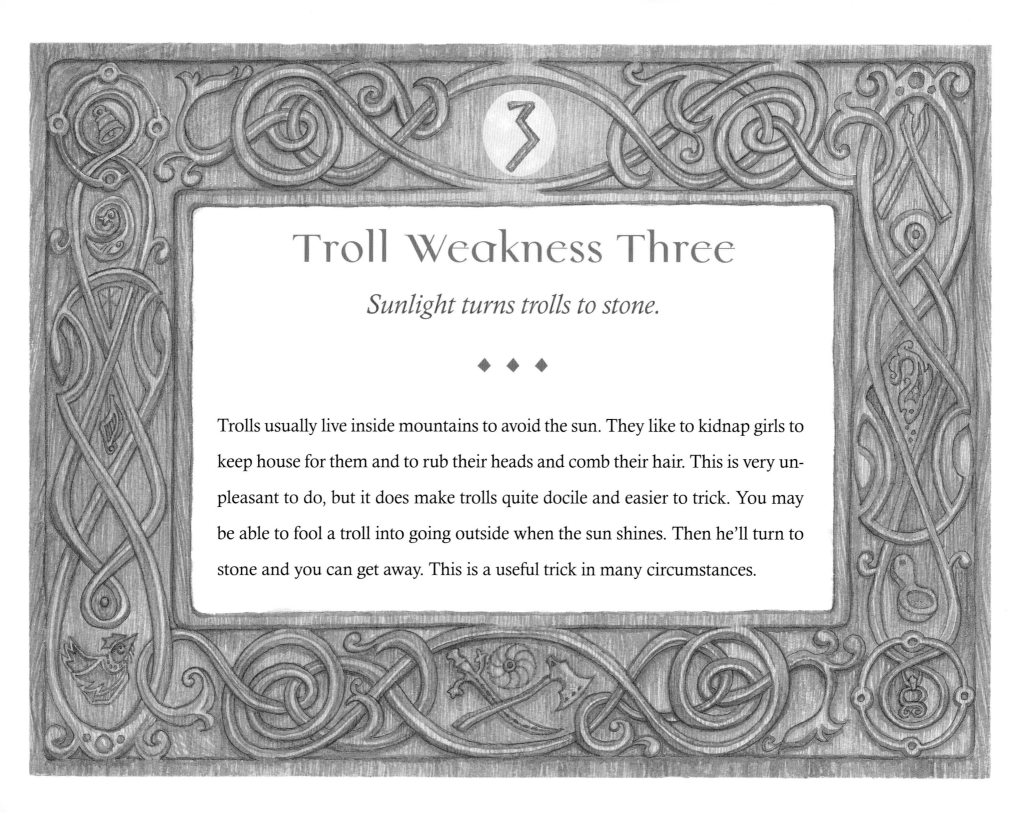

Troll Weakness Three

Sunlight turns trolls to stone.

◆ ◆ ◆

Trolls usually live inside mountains to avoid the sun. They like to kidnap girls to keep house for them and to rub their heads and comb their hair. This is very unpleasant to do, but it does make trolls quite docile and easier to trick. You may be able to fool a troll into going outside when the sun shines. Then he'll turn to stone and you can get away. This is a useful trick in many circumstances.

The Hen
Is Tripping
in the Mountain

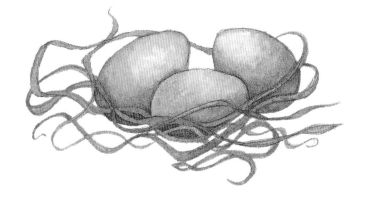

Once upon a time there was a widow who lived with her three daughters at the foot of a mountain. Their only possession was a hen, but this remarkable bird laid enough eggs to feed them and even provided extra to sell at market.

One day the hen disappeared. The widow could not find it anywhere.

"Kari, you've got to find that hen even if you have to dig her out of the mountain," she told her eldest daughter.

Kari searched and searched. Late in the afternoon she heard a gruff humming sound.

The hen is tripping in the mountain,
The hen is tripping in the mountain!

She walked toward the sound when—*snap!*—a trap door opened and she tumbled into a room filled with piles of gold and silver.

Exploring this underground world, Kari discovered room after room overflowing with treasure. Forgetting all caution, she dashed around filling her pockets with lovely jewels. In the innermost room were no jewels or treasure at all, only a mountain troll. In one hand he clutched the hen, with the other he grabbed Kari.

"I'll free the hen if you will be my sweetheart," he demanded.

"Never!" exclaimed Kari in horror.

Shaking with rage, the troll pointed his huge index finger at Kari and she turned to stone. Then he locked her in a cellar.

Back at the farm the widow called her middle daughter, Mari.

"You must look for your sister. And keep an eye out for the hen at the same time."

Mari searched up and down the mountain when she too heard
the gruff chanting.

The hen is tripping in the mountain,
The hen is tripping in the mountain!

Mari crept toward the sound when—*snap!*—
the trap door opened and she fell into the same
mountain chamber. After
searching all the rooms, she too
arrived at the innermost
chamber.

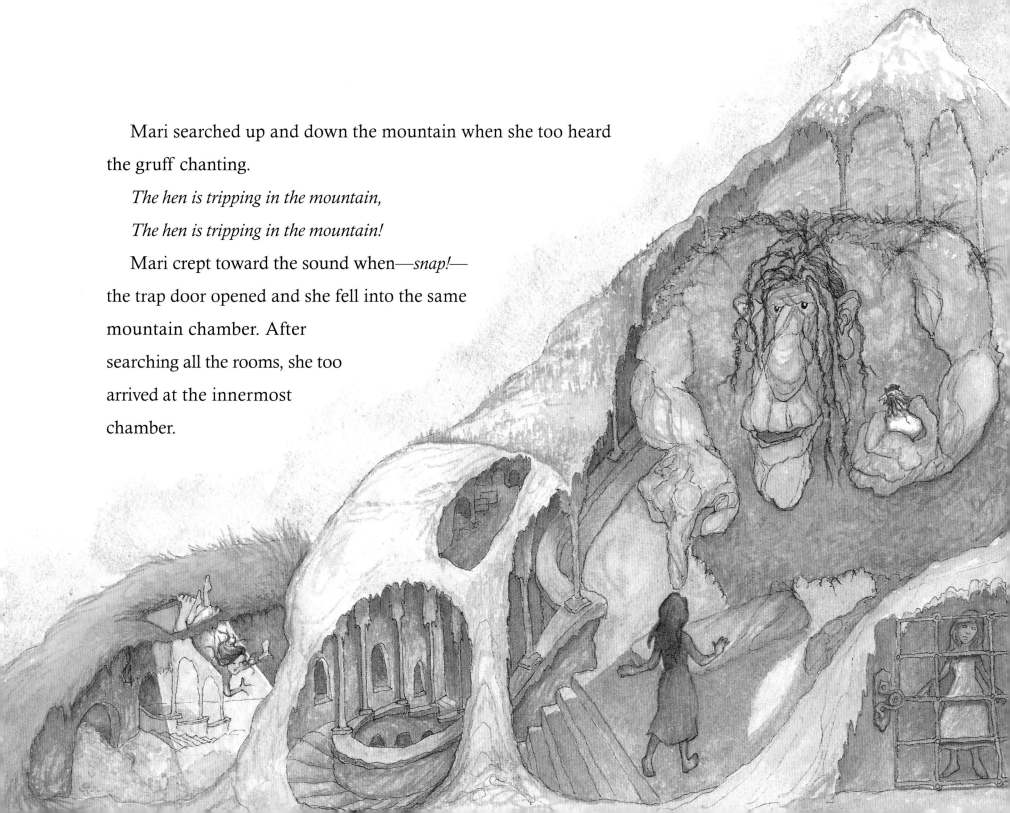

"I'll free the hen if you will be my sweetheart," demanded the troll.

Mari shook her head, so the troll turned her to stone and placed her next to her sister.

The widow waited for her daughters. Finally she said to Guri, her youngest, "Now you'll have to go look for your sisters. You can always look for the hen at the same time."

Guri searched and searched. Toward the end of the day she heard a rumbling song.

The hen is tripping in the mountain,
The hen is tripping in the mountain!

Just like her sisters, Guri fell through the trap door. But she took her time investigating the different rooms and did not touch the jewels. So much treasure could belong only to a mountain troll. As she explored she came across the cellar door and inside she saw two life-sized statues, the exact likenesses of her sisters. Now she knew what had happened.

She sauntered boldly into the last chamber where the troll sat clutching the hen.

"I'll free the hen if you will be my sweetheart," he bellowed.

"Gladly," answered Guri.

This so pleased the troll that he gave Guri everything her heart could desire: gold and silver, sparkling jewels, and dresses made of fine silks and embroidered with pearls and precious diamonds.

"The entire mountain castle is yours. Only stay away from the cellar. There is nothing there for you," he warned.

Several days passed when a billy goat fell through the trap door.

"Be gone, you silly animal," roared the troll and pointed his finger at the goat.

"Why did you do that?" complained Guri, looking at the stone animal. "I could have played with that goat."

"Don't sulk. I can bring it back to life," huffed the troll and reached for a crock, which sat half-hidden on a shelf. He rubbed ointment from the crock over the goat, and at once it shook and bleated.

Next day, as soon as the troll left, Guri grabbed the jar and hurried to the cellar. As she rubbed ointment over Kari and Mari, both came alive but trembled with fear.

"Don't worry," Guri said. "I have a plan." She placed each girl inside a trunk and fastened the locks securely. Then she put on a pretty dress and waited.

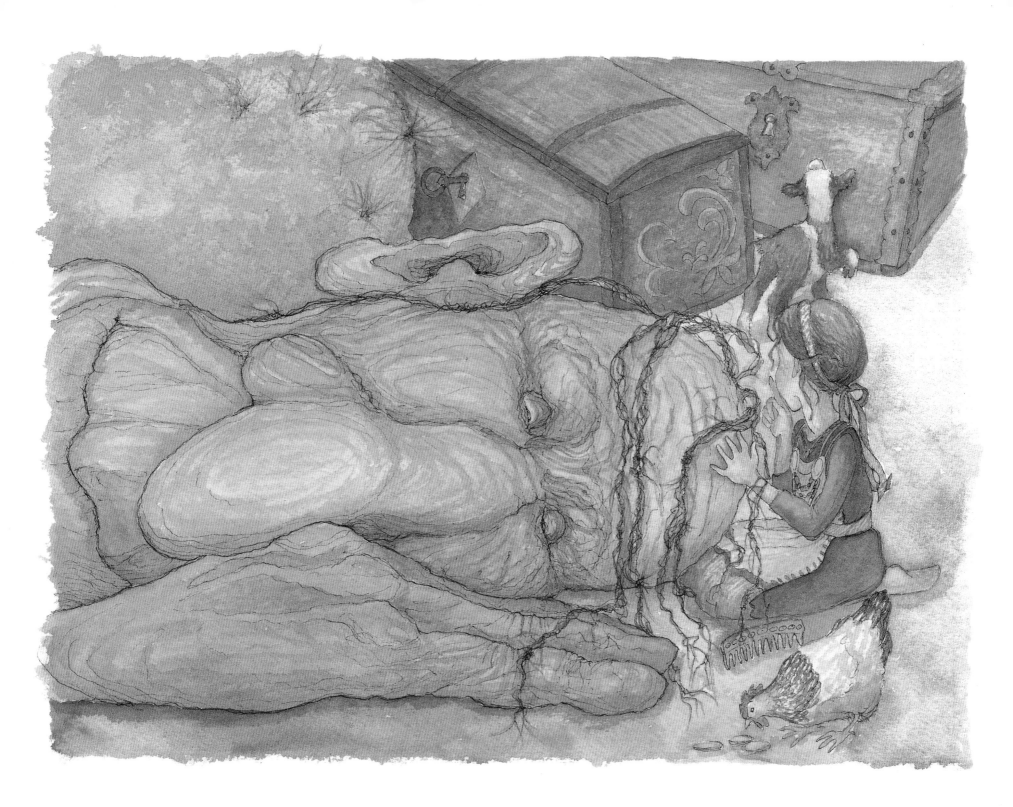

When the troll returned she smiled sweetly and said, "Dearest, you look tired and your hair is all tangled. Let me rub your head and comb your hair."

This pleased the troll, and he grew gentle.

"My dear, is there not something I can do for you in return?" he grunted.

"I have gathered some things for my mother. Will you carry this chest to her cottage this evening?" she asked sweetly. "Promise not to look inside, for I would be embarrassed if you saw the sort of silly woman's trinkets I am sending her."

The troll chuckled. He took the chest with Kari inside and carried it to the old widow's cottage. When he returned, Guri once again put his head in her lap and rubbed it until he became gentle.

"I know it made you happy to carry the chest to my mother. Will you make two more journeys for me? The chests are really not that big and my mother's need is great. If you do these errands I shall never ask for anything again. And promise not to look inside."

The troll picked up the chest with Mari.

"Supper will be ready when you are finished," called Guri as he left.

Quickly, she gathered treasures and placed them inside a third chest, leaving room on top. Then she fashioned a doll of straw, dressed it in her own clothes, and set this straw girl beside the fire. She tied a ladle to its hand so that it looked like she was cooking supper. Finally Guri climbed into the third chest.

When the troll returned he picked up the chest. But oh! This one was much heavier.

"I wonder what my sweetheart has put into this chest? I'll just take a little peek," he rumbled.

"Don't look inside. Remember, you promised me," said Guri in a voice that sounded like it was far away.

"Oh, my sweetheart can see me even in this dark," muttered the troll, and he walked on.

After a while he once again grew curious and put the chest down.

"Do not deceive me. Did you not promise you would not look?" whispered Guri.

"Oh, my sweetheart can still see me. She is far too clever," growled the troll and sped on.

As soon as he had put the chest down outside the cottage he rushed home.

"I am ravenous. Hurry with my supper!" hollered the troll. But the figure by the hearth remained motionless.

Angrily, the troll strode over and shook the figure. Straw flew all about the walls and the ceiling.

Suspicious, the troll ran to the cellar. Sure enough, the other two sisters were gone, too.

"They shall pay for this," roared the troll and rushed outside, forgetting what time it was. As soon as he stormed out of the mountain, the sun hit him in the face, and he burst into thousands of pieces of rock.

When the widow and her daughters heard the explosion, they went and fetched the hen and the goat. From that day on they lived in the greatest of happiness and comfort to the end of their lives.

Troll Weakness Four

Reflected sunshine turns trolls to stone.

◆ ◆ ◆

Trolls roam about hunting or looking for prey at night. They keep to dense and dark forests so that if the sun begins to rise while they are out, they can hide in the shadows. You can still defeat them if you use something to reflect the sun on the trolls, such as a mirror or a prism.

The Boys Who Met Trolls in the Woods

Once upon a time there was a poor couple who had so many children they couldn't feed them all. The two eldest, Evan and Erik, had to hunt and beg for food to help the family. One autumn day they did not catch a single grouse or rabbit. Tired and hungry, they set off for home. But while they walked through the woods it became dark, and they got lost.

Cutting down several sturdy pine branches, they built a small hut as a shelter for the night. They had barely settled down when they heard loud snorting and sniffing sounds. The ground trembled and a voice roared, "I smell the blood of humans!"

"Heaven help us, the trolls are out. What shall we do now?" whispered Erik.

"Let's take a look," said Evan.

A terrible sight met their eyes. Three trolls, so tall their heads were level with the treetops, stomped toward them. The troll in front had one enormous eyeball in the center of his forehead. It was as big as a frying pan, and the troll guided it with his one hand. The other trolls had a single empty eye socket in their foreheads and had to hang on to the troll in front to know where to go.

"Run out ahead of the trolls and get them to chase you. I'll take the ax and see what I can do," murmured Evan.

Erik dashed out, yelling, "Catch me if you can!"

"Brothers, there's the human! Let's capture him for our supper," hollered the first troll and took up the chase, his brothers hanging on as best they could.

Meanwhile Evan snuck up behind the last troll and whacked him in the ankle with his ax.

"Ouch, ouch!" screamed the troll, causing his brothers to topple over with fright and knocking the eyeball out of the socket. Erik picked it up and when he looked through it, he could see as clearly as though it was bright daylight. And he could see for hundreds of miles besides.

"Give me back that eyeball, or I'll eat you up right now," threatened the first troll.

"I'm not scared of you. You can't see me. I have three eyeballs now," yelled Erik.

"We'll turn you into sticks and stones if you don't give us the eyeball," warned the troll.

"I don't believe you," yelled Evan back. "If you don't watch it, I will use my ax and cut all three of you so you have to crawl on the ground like worms."

"Oh, be careful, Brother," whimpered the last troll. "He stings like an angry wasp. Please don't cut us. We'll get you gold and silver if you'll give us the eyeball back."

"Well, that sounds good," said Evan. "But I want the gold and silver before I give you the eyeball."

"We can't walk home without the eye. You have to give it to us first."

"No! Get us a bucket of gold and a bucket of silver and two good swords besides, and then we'll give you the eyeball."

The trolls grumbled, but finally the middle troll began to holler and call for their grandma, for they lived with her. The trolls told her what to do, and she arrived carrying the buckets of gold and silver and the swords. When she spotted the two boys she fumed.

"You are afraid of these little gnats. I am going to eat them for breakfast."

Holding up the eyeball, Erik yelled, "If you touch us, the eyeball will be gone forever."

"Be careful, Grandma. They're little but dangerous," warned the trolls. "Give them the gold and silver."

Snorting, she tossed the buckets and the swords over to Evan and Erik. "Now give me the eyeball," she demanded.

"Catch it if you can," yelled Erik, who tossed the eyeball straight into the air. At that very moment the sun rose. As the first rays caught the soaring eyeball, it beamed and glinted, reflecting a flash of light right at the trolls.

Kaboom! They exploded and turned to stone, all four of them. As for the eyeball, when it fell to Earth, it too turned to stone and landed on top of the heap of rocks that once had been trolls.

Then Evan and Erik picked up their swords and treasure and went home to their parents. And with all that money they lived safely and happily to the end of their days.

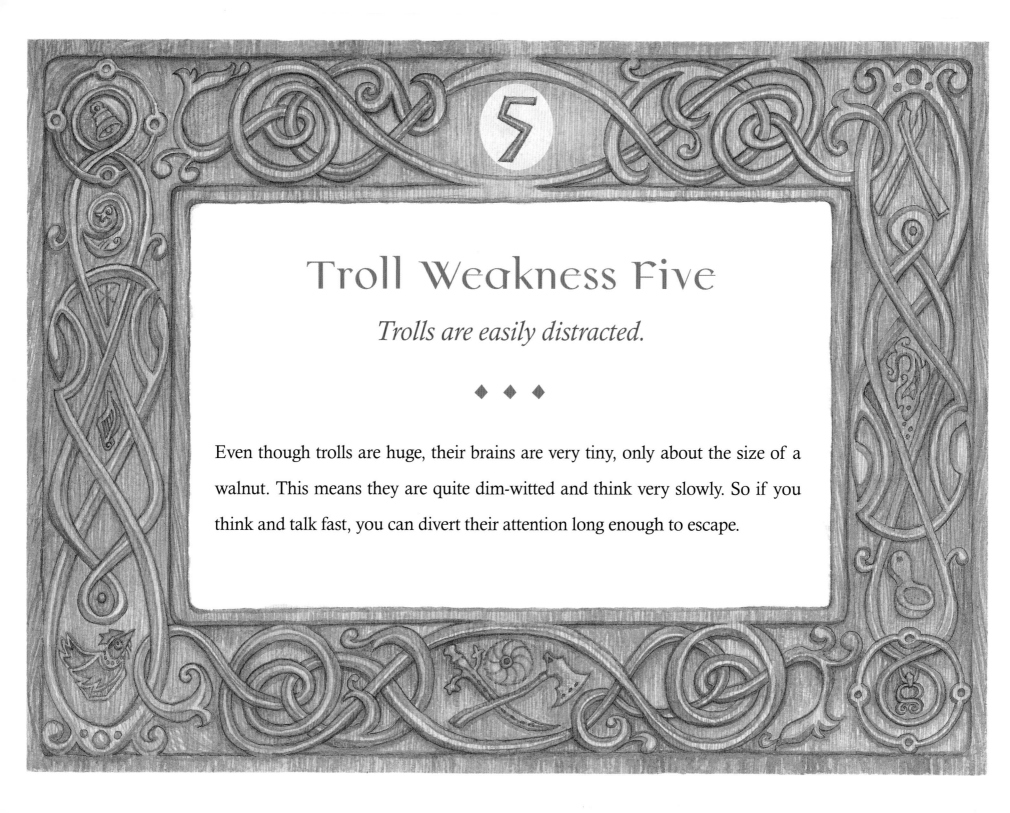

Troll Weakness Five

Trolls are easily distracted.

◆ ◆ ◆

Even though trolls are huge, their brains are very tiny, only about the size of a walnut. This means they are quite dim-witted and think very slowly. So if you think and talk fast, you can divert their attention long enough to escape.

A Narrow Escape

Once upon a time there was a small gnome with a big problem. It was the day before Christmas and Nils—that was his name—did not have a gift for his mother.

All his relatives had gathered and were cooking, talking, and laughing while Grandpa told stories to the children. Nils was only half listening until he heard Grandpa say, "For hundreds of years two trolls have stolen gold and silver from the people around here. They hide the treasure inside Mount Molnet."

Eyes sparkling, Grandpa whispered, "I have seen that treasure with my own eyes."

Nils sat bolt upright.

"High up on the north side of Mount Molnet is a door. It opens into the mountain, but it is so heavy that only a troll can move it, except on Christmas Eve. Then the door swings open all by itself. But it slams shut again when the bells ring on Christmas morning. I barely escaped," Grandpa added with a grin.

Nils's heart thumped. A piece of treasure was the perfect present for his mom. And tonight the door would swing open.

As soon as everyone slept, Nils slipped outside and strapped on his skis. Up and up he skied through dense pine forest until the trees thinned and a rock wall loomed in front of him. A faint glow shimmered on one side. Nils skied closer and saw a huge door, slightly open, just as Grandpa had said.

Leaving his skis and poles in the snow, Nils crept through the door. Inside flickering torches lit up an immense hall and right in the middle sat a chest as big as a wagon. A troll and a hag stood hunched over the chest admiring their treasure.

The troll hag's nose was so long it touched the ground in front of her. Now it began to quiver.

"I smell something," she sniffled, lifting her enormous snout.

"I don't smell anything," snuffled the troll.

"Smell again," snorted the hag, and both trolls sucked air in so deeply that a whirlwind of dust flew up and into their noses.

"Aahhchooo!" went the trolls and fell back from the force of the sneezes.

The blast picked up Nils and whisked him through the air like a leaf, dropping him smack into the trunk.

Bracelets, brooches, rings, coins, candlesticks, and goblets glittered around him.

One slender necklace with a red stone sparkled and twinkled more beautifully than the rest. It would be lovely around his mother's neck, thought Nils. He grabbed the necklace and crawled to the edge of the chest, ready to jump.

"Ding, dong," chimed the bells of Christmas morning.

"Thunk," went the door to the mountain.

"Thud," went the lid of the chest.

Nils was trapped. But he was not afraid.

"Peep, peep, peep," he squeaked through the keyhole.

"What was that?" yelped the troll.

"There's a mouse in the trunk!" cried the hag.

"Oh, leave it to starve. It won't eat our gold."

"It might chew a hole in the trunk," complained the hag.

"No, it won't," growled the troll.

"Yes, it will."

"No, it won't."

"Yes, I will," piped up Nils from inside the trunk.

The trolls looked at each other, then at the trunk.

"Well, open it," the hag snapped.

"Ha ha! What a funny-looking mouse," guffawed the troll when he spotted Nils.

"I'm not a mouse. I am a gnome," declared Nils, hands on his hips.

"Yum! He'll make fine stuffing for the Christmas goose," screeched the hag and went to the kitchen.

Folding his arms Nils said firmly, "You can't eat me. I'm too dirty."

"You look clean enough to me," objected the troll.

"No, no. Look here," said Nils and held out his hands, filthy from crawling on the floor. "You'll need to wash me first."

"I guess you're right," admitted the troll and carried Nils to a pool.

Now this pool was part of an underground river.

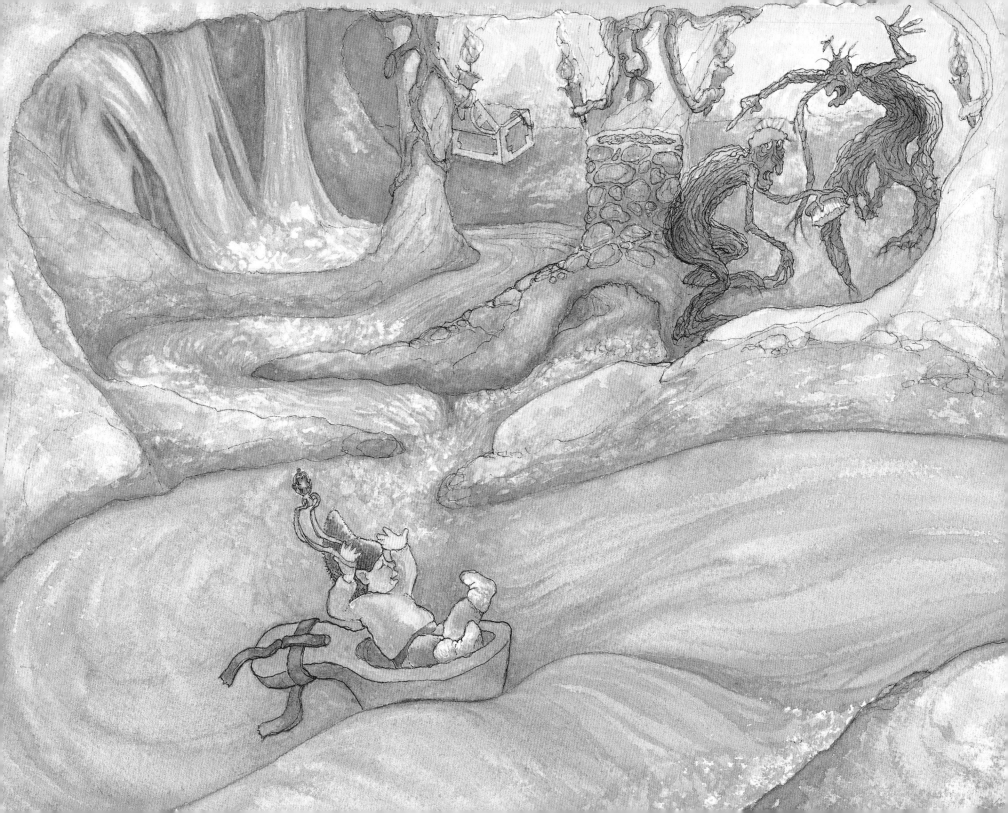

Water flowed in at one side and disappeared out a hole at the other end.

A large wooden cup that the trolls used for drinking hung by a piece of rope from a hook.

The troll splashed water on Nils.

"Now you're clean," he declared.

"You'll need both a brush and some soap to scrub away all this grime," insisted Nils.

Grumbling, the troll set Nils down at the edge of the well and went to fetch cleaning supplies.

As soon as the troll turned his back, Nils leaped into the wooden cup. He fished out his pocketknife and started to cut the cord. He sawed and he sliced, but the rope was very thick, and he had not quite cut through when the trolls spotted him.

"Stop!" they roared and sprinted toward the well.

Just as the trolls reached him, the cup dropped into the water.

Down the river sailed Nils, around sharp curves and over jagged boulders till the river shot out of the mountain. The cup hit the riverbank and hurled Nils into a big, soft snowbank right by his farm.

That Christmas, Nils had two presents for his mom: a lovely necklace and a story as good as any that Grandpa could tell about how to trick the trolls in the mountain.

Troll Weakness Six

Trolls cannot swim.

◆ ◆ ◆

Even though trolls are tall and can wade across shallow lakes, they dislike open water because they cannot swim. You can use this information in many different ways.

The Troll
Who Played
Hide-and-Go-Seek

Once upon a time a boy named Lars went into the forest to chop wood for his family. When he had filled his sack, he sat down to eat. Just as he was unwrapping his sandwich, a tiny dwarf with a long silver beard appeared in front of him.

"Could you spare a few coins for a poor old soul so I can buy some food?" begged the dwarf.

"I have no money. But I'll be happy to share with you," said Lars and gave half of his lunch to the dwarf. The little man gobbled the sandwich so quickly that Lars handed him his bottle as well. The dwarf gulped half the contents before handing it back. Then he snapped his fingers and disappeared.

"And not one word of thanks!" exclaimed Lars, surprised.

Grabbing the firewood, he set off for home. He had scarcely taken five steps when a troll came crashing through the woods. This troll was so big that his head was taller than the treetops. One single eye in the middle of his forehead glared at Lars.

"How dare you chop in my woods!" roared the troll. "Now I'm going to gobble you up."

"Oh, please don't eat me," begged Lars. "My family will never survive without my help. I'm the oldest of seven children."

"I don't care," snorted the troll. "But I'm not hungry right now, so let's play hide-and-go-seek. I can only eat you if I find you. Now run!" bellowed the troll. He slapped a huge hand over his eyeball and began to count, "1, 5, 3, 2 . . ."

Lars looked under bushes and behind rocks, but no place seemed like a clever hiding spot. All at once the dwarf with the silver beard appeared.

"Come with me," he whispered and guided Lars to a large oak. The dwarf cut a huge splint out of the tree trunk. "Crawl in," he urged and pushed Lars into the space. Then he placed the splinter on top and closed up the tree trunk.

"62, 83, 34, 100. Ready or not, here I come!" yelled the troll. Sniffing the air he ran straight to the tree where Lars was hiding. He squeezed his eyeball.

"Aha!" he roared and toppled the tree with one tremendous swing of his ax. "Found you!" he hollered triumphantly and pulled Lars out of his hiding place.

"This is fun! I'm not hungry yet, so hide once more."

The troll slapped his hand over the eye and counted, "1, 7, 3, 2 . . ."

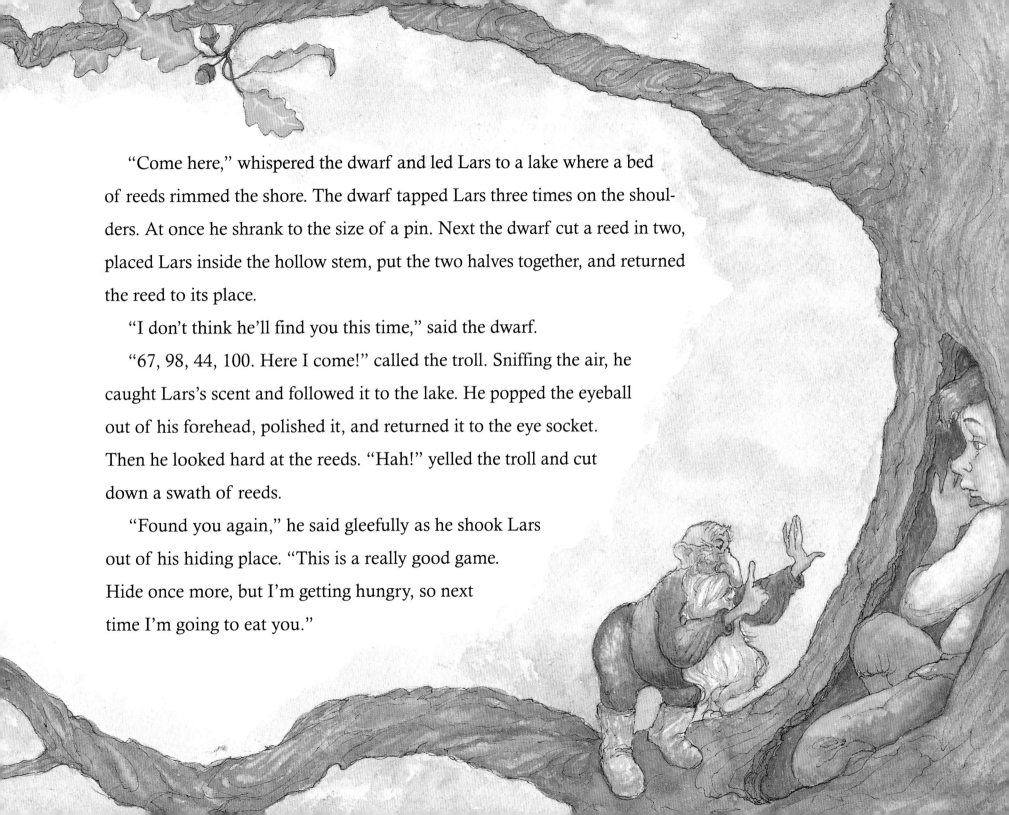

"Come here," whispered the dwarf and led Lars to a lake where a bed of reeds rimmed the shore. The dwarf tapped Lars three times on the shoulders. At once he shrank to the size of a pin. Next the dwarf cut a reed in two, placed Lars inside the hollow stem, put the two halves together, and returned the reed to its place.

"I don't think he'll find you this time," said the dwarf.

"67, 98, 44, 100. Here I come!" called the troll. Sniffing the air, he caught Lars's scent and followed it to the lake. He popped the eyeball out of his forehead, polished it, and returned it to the eye socket. Then he looked hard at the reeds. "Hah!" yelled the troll and cut down a swath of reeds.

"Found you again," he said gleefully as he shook Lars out of his hiding place. "This is a really good game. Hide once more, but I'm getting hungry, so next time I'm going to eat you."

"What shall we do?" Lars asked the dwarf. "With that nose he can smell me and with that eyeball he can see everything."

"I have one more idea," said the dwarf. He bent down and whistled three times over the water. A red fish swam to the surface and the dwarf caught it. He broke the fish in two and placed Lars, who was still tiny, inside.

"The rest is up to you," whispered the dwarf. He joined the two parts of the fish and threw it into the lake.

"Ready or not, here I come!" thundered the troll. "Make way, for I am hungry and plan to catch my supper."

At the lake he sniffed the air and scanned the water. The little red fish swam to the surface.

"I see you!" roared the troll and lifted his spear. But the fish disappeared in the deep.

Searching the shore, the troll found an enormous hollowed-out log, which he put into the lake. He climbed inside, and using his hands as oars he paddled out to the middle of the lake. Twisting and

turning the eyeball,

he peered into the green water. Suddenly

the little fish popped up on one side of the log.

   "Now I've got you!" yelled the troll and

lifted his spear.

   But the little fish, with Lars directing it, darted

underneath the log and came up on the other side.

The troll flung himself around, his spear high.

Again, the fish slipped beneath the log and popped

up on the other side. He kept swimming from one

side to the other, and the troll swiveled back

and forth so fast that the log began to

rock and tilt. All at once it rolled over and

the troll toppled into the lake. And

he sank like a rock to the bottom,

for trolls cannot swim.

Now the dwarf whistled three times and the
little red fish swam to the surface. He caught it,
broke it in two, lifted Lars out, and restored him
to his proper size. Then he put the fish together
and tossed it back into the lake, where it swam
away with a merry swish of its tail.

"Thank you for saving my life," gasped Lars.

"And thank you for sharing your lunch," said the dwarf. Then he snapped his fingers and vanished.

Lars never saw the dwarf again, but he spent many happy hours telling his family about the adventure he had with the troll with the single eyeball and the dwarf with the silver beard. ◌

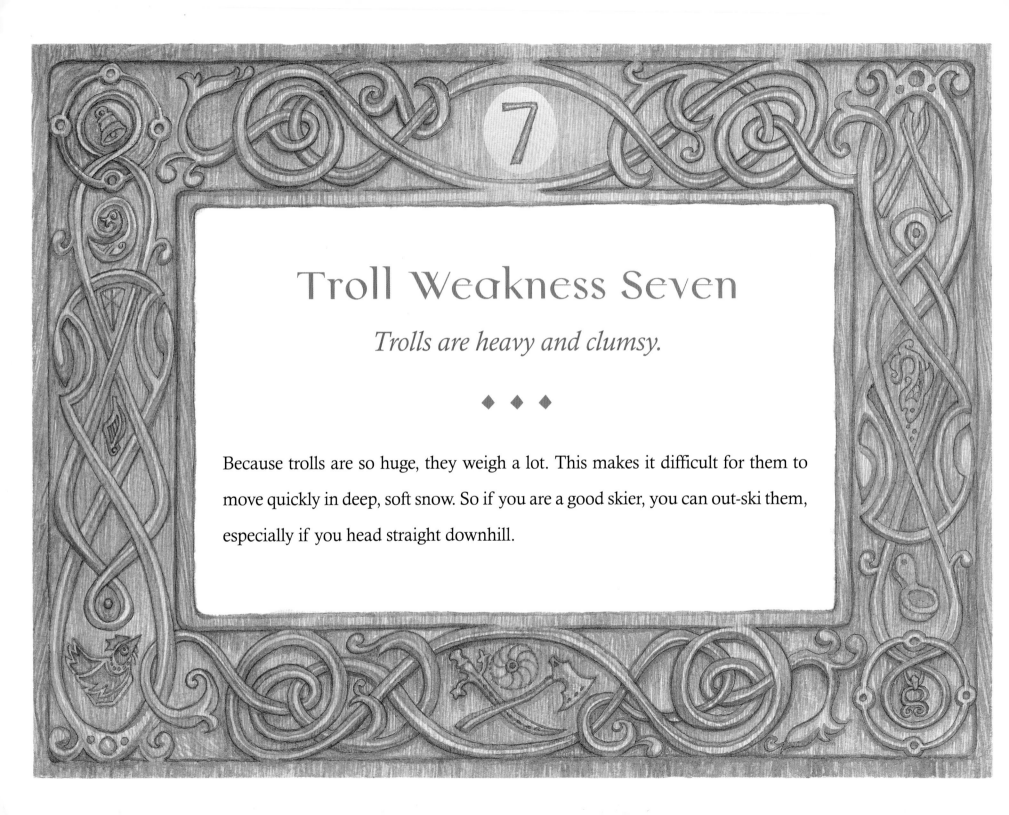

Troll Weakness Seven

Trolls are heavy and clumsy.

◆ ◆ ◆

Because trolls are so huge, they weigh a lot. This makes it difficult for them to move quickly in deep, soft snow. So if you are a good skier, you can out-ski them, especially if you head straight downhill.

Tor Out-Skis the Trolls

Once upon a time there was a boy named Tor who was very wild. Every chance he got, he ran off into the mountains to fish and hunt. No matter how hard his family begged him to stay and work on the farm, after a few weeks at home he would slip away.

One winter evening, Tor had been away for several days when he spotted a fire burning inside a mountain.

Curious to see who else was making camp, he skied toward the light. As he drew closer he heard grunts and slipped behind a fir tree to listen.

"Can I borrow that big cauldron of yours?" rumbled a troll voice.

"What do you want a cauldron for?" grumbled another.

"I'm going to catch that boy Tor and then I'm going to cook him."

Smacking his fat lips, the second troll growled. "You can have the cauldron but only if I can have some Tor to eat, too!"

Tor's heart thumped and his legs shook. He did not want to become troll stew. Quietly, he pushed his skis through the snow and headed downhill. He was just beginning to pick up a little speed when—*thwack!*—his skis snagged on a buried spruce branch and he toppled over.

"Who's sneaking around out there?" bellowed the first troll.

"It's Tor!" hollered the second troll, pointing. "Let's get him," urged the first troll, and he set off so fast that he started a small avalanche. Tor scrambled up, grabbed his poles, and pointed his skis straight downhill. He shot down a steep ravine, raced between trees, and jumped off cliffs. The trolls roared in fury as they saw him glide down the mountain.

But they kept up the chase. With their excellent night vision they easily saw him outlined against the white snow and even though his skis were fast, they wouldn't stop.

Tor pushed on, heading for the valley and his village, which lay across from a lake. If he skied around the lake, the trolls might catch up with him. He'd have to ski across.

He tested the ice and thought, "This is thick enough for a light boy like me. But those two trolls are awfully heavy. I wonder . . ."

Turning toward the pursuing trolls, he called, "Catch me if you can!"

Then he skied straight out onto the lake.

"Ho ho! We'll get him now," roared the trolls and pounded after him.

The ice creaked.

Tor stopped and stuck out his tongue. "You'll never get me! I'm faster than you are!" he taunted and continued toward the middle of the lake.

Shaking their fists, the trolls doubled their effort. Their fur-covered feet and clawed toes gripped the snow and ice, and soon they thundered right behind Tor. He felt their hot breath down his neck as they lunged after him.

Quick as a rabbit, Tor leaped to the side and out of the trolls' reach. They flew forward and landed, THUNK.

CRACK, went the ice and broke open. The trolls sank through the hole and down to the bottom of the lake. And there they stayed, for as you know, trolls cannot swim!

Tor hurried home as fast as his skis would carry him. When he arrived at the farm, he saw candles burning in all the windows and remembered it was Christmas Eve.

His parents wept for joy when he told them of his narrow escape. They said that having him home safely was the best Christmas gift they had ever received.

Tor never ran away to the mountains again, and don't you do that either.

How to Spot a Troll

By now you know that trolls have become extinct, at least as far as we know. But that does not mean you cannot see trolls. Their remains can be found everywhere if you just know how to look. So the next time you are in the woods, in the mountains, or by lakes or oceans, use these guidelines and start looking for trolls!

1. To find remnants of trolls that burst and turned to stone, you need to look carefully at rocks. Sometimes all you have to do is to look at the shape of a mountain or certain hills, and you will see it is a troll caught by the rising sun. In the Nordic countries there are so many mountains named after the trolls they once were that I can hardly count them all. One good example in North America is Sleeping Giant Peninsula in Canada. From a distance you clearly see that it is a troll who was sleeping on his back when the sun came out. I think Giant's Ridge in northern Minnesota is another such place. Can you find others?

2. Many islands are actually trolls caught wading from one place to another when the sun rose. The coast between Norway and Iceland is full of these dead trolls. The trick is to look at the shape of an island from a distance. Can you see the troll?

3. Because trolls cannot swim, they often lingered too long by shores thinking of ways to cross the water safely. Many got caught by the sun's early rays and—*boom!*—exploded. As a result, lakes and oceans are good spots to find troll remains. My son found a troll's eyeball in Lake Superior when he was seven. Besides eyeballs, you may be able to find troll brains (about the size of a walnut), fingers, toes, ears, and even noses. Troll rocks are exceptionally smooth and often feel a little different in your hand. Some sparkle. Hold the rock, rub it, and look carefully at the shape. With practice, you will be able to tell if it's part of a troll or just an ordinary rock.

4. As trolls age, they begin to shrink and become more and more stooped. Because they never wash, layers of dirt settle on their backs and head, and over time bushes and even small trees grow up. Then they begin to petrify. In the end trolls become so stiff that they take only a step or two a year, until they petrify completely. You will find these trolls in deep forests (they survived so long by keeping away from sunny clearings), and they strongly resemble overturned tree roots. Look closely and you may be able to see the eye sockets and noses. Often the arms protrude at odd angles. Some parts may have broken off over time, but with practice you will be able to spot which roots are dead trolls and which are just ordinary tree roots. ✍

Sources

Little Goose

Many brief anecdotes tell how trolls hate noise, particularly the sound of church bells. For example, this joke: one day a troll who lived in a mountain shouted, "There's a cow bellowing!" Seven years later the troll who lived across the valley answered, "Couldn't it just as well be a bull as a cow?" Another seven years passed before a troll in a third mountain screamed, "If you two don't keep quiet and stop this commotion, I'll have to move!" I have never been able to find a longer story about trolls who hate noise, but one day I read a Japanese folktale, "The Terrible Black Snake's Revenge," in *The Sea of Gold and Other Tales from Japan,* by Yoshiko Uchida. Using that tale as a blueprint and my knowledge of trolls and their characteristics, I wrote "Little Goose."

The Ashlad Who Stole the Troll's Treasures

This story is from Peter Christen Asbjørnsen and Jørgen Engebretsen Moe, "Askeladden Som Stjal Sølvendene til Trollet." After years of oral storytelling, I made some changes to this tale. I added that the objects the Ashlad steals from the troll originally belonged to the king's family. Norwegian children already know this kind of cultural knowledge, so there is no mention of it in the Asbjørnsen story. I wanted American children to know that the king wasn't a common thief.

The Hen Is Tripping in the Mountain

This tale from Asbjørnsen and Moe, "Høna som Tripper i Berget," is a Norwegian variant on a story well known in other European countries, such as "Jurma and the Sea Monster" from Finland (in *Scandinavian Folk and Fairy Tales,* edited by Claire Booss). The Norwegian version has all the classic characteristics of a great troll story, full of delicious suspense and with an excellent resolution.

The Boys Who Met Trolls in the Woods

This is one of Asbjørnsen and Moe's best-known stories, "Guttene Som Møtte Trollet i Heddal Skogen." My telling is fairly faithful to the original except for a few changes that crept in after thirty years of oral storytelling. For instance, in the Norwegian story the sun rises over the trees, causing the trolls to burst. Since anything that reflects sunlight will also cause them to burst, I thought it more empowering, and more fun, to have one of the boys toss the eyeball into the air, and then have the eyeball catch and reflect the sun's rays onto the trolls. This can inspire lively discussions about other objects that can reflect sunlight and destroy the trolls.

A Narrow Escape

This story is from an old Swedish Christmas magazine, *Bland Tomtar och Troll (Among Gnomes and Trolls)*. It has been published every year since 1907, and several of Sweden's foremost authors and illustrators have worked for the annual. This particular story was written by Alfred Smedberg in 1909 and was called "Trollen och Tomte Pojken" ("The Trolls and the Gnome Boy"). The original was much longer, including a lengthy frame story. I focused on the inside story and tightened it considerably, though it retains the traditional theme of the gentle little gnome against the big, hungry, mean trolls.

The Troll Who Played Hide-and-Go-Seek

The source for my retelling is a story called "Nils in the Forest" in *A Book of Ogres and Trolls,* by Ruth Manning-Sanders, who declares that the story is of Danish origin.

Trolls' fear of water is well documented. Despite this, some especially tall trolls have waded across the ocean all the way to Iceland and Greenland—and probably to North America as well. They followed ridges in the ocean. Some trolls stumbled and drowned; others were still out when the sun rose and turned to stone. They became islands off the coasts of the Nordic countries. It is possible many islands off the coast of Newfoundland and Labrador are dead trolls, too. I have always been curious if they made it all the way to Ontario and northern Minnesota. Sleeping Giant Peninsula outside Thunder Bay, Ontario, looks like a troll caught napping when the sun came out. And there's Giant's Ridge in Minnesota . . . with a name like that, one wonders.

Tor Out-Skis the Trolls

The base of this story, "Trolls Resent a Disturbance," is found in Reidar Christiansen's *Folktales of Norway,* a fabulous collection of strange and haunting stories. I first used a skeleton outline of this tale to teach children about writing and storytelling. Over the years I have told it many times, adding and subtracting details with the help of children. This is my most recent version.

Other books that I love for their odd and curious anecdotes about trolls and hidden folk are *Scandinavian Folktales,* translated and edited by Jacqueline Simpson (Penguin Books, 1988); *Scandinavian Folk Belief and Legend,* edited by Reimund Kvideland and Henning K. Sehmsdorf (University of Minnesota Press, 1988); *The Fairy Mythology, Illustrative of the Romance and Superstition of Various Countries,* by Thomas Keightley (Crown Publishers, 1880); and my all-time favorite, *Scandinavian Folk-Lore: Illustrations of the Traditional Beliefs of the Northern Peoples,* selected and translated by William A. Craigie (Alexander Gardner, 1896).

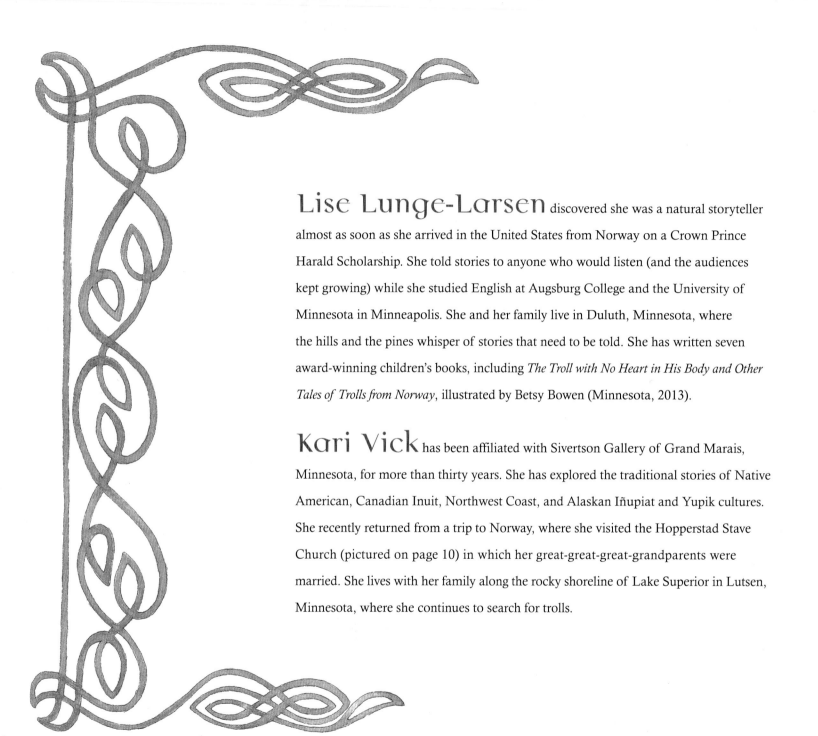

Lise Lunge-Larsen discovered she was a natural storyteller almost as soon as she arrived in the United States from Norway on a Crown Prince Harald Scholarship. She told stories to anyone who would listen (and the audiences kept growing) while she studied English at Augsburg College and the University of Minnesota in Minneapolis. She and her family live in Duluth, Minnesota, where the hills and the pines whisper of stories that need to be told. She has written seven award-winning children's books, including *The Troll with No Heart in His Body and Other Tales of Trolls from Norway*, illustrated by Betsy Bowen (Minnesota, 2013).

Kari Vick has been affiliated with Sivertson Gallery of Grand Marais, Minnesota, for more than thirty years. She has explored the traditional stories of Native American, Canadian Inuit, Northwest Coast, and Alaskan Iñupiat and Yupik cultures. She recently returned from a trip to Norway, where she visited the Hopperstad Stave Church (pictured on page 10) in which her great-great-great-grandparents were married. She lives with her family along the rocky shoreline of Lake Superior in Lutsen, Minnesota, where she continues to search for trolls.